The UniCORn and the Wild HORses

Written by Claire Philip   Illustrated by Sandra Aguilar

Miles Kelly

Luna the unicorn lived
with a herd of wild horses.

She had appeared during a
flurry of shooting stars.

"She'll bring trouble!" grumbled some of the horses.
Yet one of the older mares said Luna could stay.

As she was growing up, the other foals teased Luna. They would make fun of her horn.

Luna didn't understand why they were so mean.

She spent most of her time on her own.

Luna daydreamed about what it would be like to find a herd of horses just like her.

One day, Luna wandered far from her herd.
It was winter, and snowing heavily.

Unlike the other horses, Luna didn't feel
the cold. She lay down and fell asleep.

As Luna slept, the herd left the plains to cross the snowy mountain pass to look for food.

The horses set off, and poor Luna was left behind!

Luna had a dream about a
beautiful forest.

She knew she was asleep,
yet it felt so real!

In her dream, a blue **hummingbird** hovered in front of her before darting off.

She also saw a trail of sparkling fireflies in between the trees.

In her dream, Luna walked over to them. She saw that the fireflies lit up a path.

Slowly, she walked along it. Quite soon, she heard neighing.

She entered a clearing and saw a group of horses that looked like her!

"Welcome Luna!" one called.

"We are your true herd. You aren't a horse... you are a unicorn!"

"What do you mean?" asked Luna.

"Well, you are one hundred times as strong as a horse. Your horn can send out beams of sunlight, too."

"And you can also arrive in a new place simply by imagining you are already there."

"Point your horn at these logs, and imagine them burning," said one of the unicorns.

Luna did this, and suddenly the wood began to burn.

"Wow!" Luna cried.

"Now lift this fallen tree with your horn."

Luna placed her horn just under the tree, and as she stood up the tree moved too!

"Can I live here?" Luna asked.
She felt very happy.

"You can come here each night, but during the day you must protect your herd," said the friendly unicorn.

"But they are unkind to me," said Luna, sadly.

"They need your help right now, Luna! They are trapped by heavy snow!"

Luna didn't want to go, but she couldn't leave her herd in danger.

"I will help them," she said.

"Close your eyes, say 'wake up',
and you'll be back at home,"
said her new friend.

Luna did as she was asked, and
woke up back on the plains,
surrounded by snow.

Immediately, Luna imagined herself at the pass. She felt a whooshing feeling and then she was on the move!

When Luna arrived she saw a huge pile of snow blocking the pass.

Luna pointed her horn at the snow. A beam of light burst out and melted it all away!

Then she saw a mound of rocks blocking the way.

Using her horn, she moved them one by one.

"Luna, you saved us," cried one of the horses. "We are so sorry we were mean."

Luna smiled. "Let's start again and be friends."

From then on, Luna spent the days with her herd and the nights with her unicorn family.